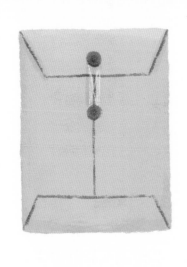
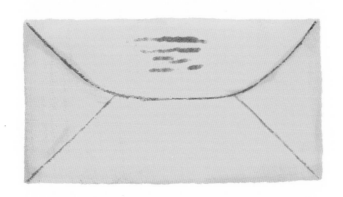

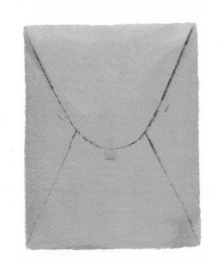

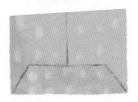

dear UNICORN

written by **Josh Funk**

illustrated by **Charles Santoso**

VIKING

VIKING
An imprint of Penguin Random House LLC, New York

First published in the United States of America by Viking, an imprint of Penguin Random House LLC, 2023

Text copyright © 2023 by Josh Funk
Illustrations copyright © 2023 by Charles Santoso

Visit us online at PenguinRandomHouse.com.

Library of Congress Cataloging-in-Publication Data is available.

Manufactured in China

ISBN 9780593206942

10 9 8 7 6 5 4 3 2 1

TOPL

Design by Kate Renner
Text set in Ionic No 5, Harimau Dua, and Glitter Candy

The artwork for this book was created using digital brushes in Photoshop.

September 2
Dear Nicole Sharp,

I feel a little weird putting art in the mail.
This project seems a bit sketchy. I've always
felt art belongs in museums and galleries.
Also, I have disastrous news: it's the first
day of school and my best friend, Raven,
isn't in my class. Could it get any worse?

I'm supposed to ask you questions. What's
your favorite color? Today mine is blue.

Sincerely,
Constance Nace-Ayre

October 11
Dear Constance Nace-Ayre,

Art and letters sound delightful! Although I'm not a huge fan of museums. They're so stuffy. And you can't touch ANYTHING.

I'm sorry you're not in Raven's class. My best friend, Misty, is in a different class, too. But we still eat lunch together every day. Yesterday I spent all day baking for her birthday. When's your birthday?

Cordially yours,
Nicole Sharp
P.S. If you haven't already guessed, my favorite color is also BLUE!

- CNA -

November 1
Dear Nicole Sharp,

All day baking?! Ugh. I had to do chores
all day yesterday, too. Last week my soccer
team lost in the championship by one goal!
Can you believe it?!

My birthday is July 21st, so I never get
to celebrate in school. When's yours?

From Constance (but everyone just
calls me "Connie")

December 1
Dear Connie,

Wow! You made the championship! And almost won? Congrats! My birthday is Leap Day, February 29th. I only get to celebrate every four years. But when I do, it's the BEST PARTY EVER!

Bad news—I broke my horn! It's gonna take six weeks to mend it. On the bright side, I have more time for art. Like my dad always says, "Life is all glitter and cupcakes if you look at it right!"

Question: What's your favorite book?

Yours truly,
Nicole (but my friends call me "Nic")

December 21
Dear Nicole,

Sorry about your horn. I take clarinet lessons
every Tuesday.

I love learning about history. I just finished a book
called <u>Art: The Good, the Bad, and the Medieval.</u>
What do you like to read?

Yesterday my moms made me help out at the
animal shelter. Can you imagine being around cats
all . . . day . . . long . . . ?

Connie
P.S. I hope you're not allergic. Hair and fur
might be in the paint.

January 21
Dear Connie,

I am SOOO jealous! You got to hang out with cute fluffy kittens! I love the spots and stripes and colors! Isn't Mother Nature the most magical artist of all?

I love nonfiction, too! My favorite series is Mystical Treasure Hunters. You should totally check it out.

Did you go anywhere over winter break? I visited my friend Abe in the mountains. We love rolling giant snowballs into men.

Nic
P.S. Your art is always gorgeous. I was wondering, though . . . have you ever tried drawing cartoons?

February 29
Nic,

Happy birthday!

For vacation we went to Sparky's World, the amusement park. I went on all the rides EXCEPT the Flying Dragons. I was ONE INCH too short.

Thanks for suggesting the Mystical Treasure Hunters. I didn't see the twist at the end of book #1 coming at all! And I never asked, do you play any sports?

Your friend,
Connie
P.S. Your pictures are great, too. They always cheer me up.

March 26
Connie,

Sparky's World looks exciting! And now you've got something fun to look forward to next time (although I've heard flying on dragons isn't really all that great).

As far as sports, I like to run. I have a race today. Here's a picture of me hoofing it so fast, I'm a blur (not that I can predict the future or anything).

Did you hear about the Pen Pal Art Festival? And we're gonna share our art with everyone? I'm not sure mine is "gallery-worthy," though.

Your friend,
Nic
P.S. Just wait until the twist at the end of book #2!

TOP SECRET

April 17
Hey, Nic,

I hope you ~~won~~ had fun at your track meet.
I'm super thrilled about the Pen Pal Art
Festival! I can't wait to meet in real life! I
heard there will even be a bouncy castle.

I absolutely love your artwork. It might seem
corny, but I've hung it all around my room.

Also . . . I have a secret idea for the festival
I think you might like.

Your pal,
Connie
P.S. Use the Treasure Hunters' invisible ink
trick to read the secret.

May 5
Hey, Connie,

Most castles I know are made of stone. I've never been to a bouncy one. And I also framed your artwork. I'm staring at it now!

And I'm 100% on board with your secret idea. Let's meet at the Pen Pal Art Festival two hours early. See you there.

Your bud,
Nic

P.S. You might recognize this castle from page 394 of Art: The Good, the Bad, and the Medieval.

*Dear Percy, I can't wait to see what you
create next (even though sometimes the waiting
is the best part). Love, Dad —J. F.*

*To the SG PB group,
thank you for the fun Wednesdays. —C. S.*

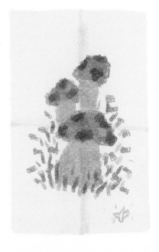